When Dracula met the Jabberwocky

By Paul Fitz-George

**The old graveyard at St Mary's the Virgin
overlooking the harbour**

Note. A very big thank you to all the young Goths and Steampunks appearing in this book's pages, who kindly posed for these pictures whilst they were attending one of Whitby's great Goth Weekends. Their enthusiastic poses will, I hope, help set the scene for the stories about the famous Victorian authors we will discuss and who like them, promenaded along Whitby's old cobbled streets over a century before.

Some very pretty Steampunk and Goth gels who would most certainly have had the hats of our illustrious authors doffed to them, had they graced Whitby's Streets in the late 19th century

My crown is called content;

A crown it is that that seldom kings enjoy.

'3 Henry VI 3.1.64 -5'

Table of Contents

Foreword

The sentinel East and West Lighthouses that guard the harbour's mouth

Whitby, as you approach it from the high cliff-top on which lies that ancient 13th century Benedictine Abbey and stately Abbey House, appears to the observer to be a typical eighteenth century seaport. In appearance, it's too big for a village, but just a bit too small for what could be called a town. At one point in time though, it was one of the biggest ship building ports in England and it was here that Captain Cook's famous ship Endeavour was built. It was also once a major east coast whaling port, until both these industries (fortunately for our beloved whales) died out.

Whitby's narrow streets have paid host to the Celts, Romans, Anglo Saxons, Viking raiders and finally the conquering Normans. First came the Celt Parisi tribe from the Marne in France, who eventually came under Rome's imperial rule and the commanding stare of its legate Petillius Cerialis in AD 71-73. Empire's rise and fall, Rome sadly departing our shores when the empire imploded hastening in the warrior Chief Soemic, an Anglo Saxon from the nearby kingdom of Deira, who gave the town the name of Streonshalh. His descendants were in turn subjected to the terror of the Viking raiders from Denmark. They named the town 'Whitby' (literally 'the white town') and gave it a parliament or Thingwala just like the one in Iceland, at which point in time the town's name was stabilised much to the relief of 'yea ancient mapmakers'.

It was not however the end of the land acquisition business, as along came those well known historical achievers the Normans, in the form of one William de Percy. He was also known as 'Aux Gernons' or 'with whiskers', this nickname bringing the forename Algernon into the Percy family, the English language and to be used later by typical English writers like P G Woodhouse.

All was not over on the armed robbery front however, as in the 1150's the King of Norway Eystein II, had a sulk and for his amusement decided to sack the town, but didn't stay. Thankfully and from then on barring the odd pirate raid, things quietened down on the invasion front and Whitby's citizens could at last step out of their houses without the immediate fear of being perforated by axe, arrow or sword, whew!

Gradually, the town began to prosper in both the ship building and whaling industries, the wealth from which eventually drying up in the nineteenth century, leaving fishing and tourism as the town's main source of income…and ghosts and the supernatural of course!

A young Goth in Victorian attire

It is not surprising with this troubled background then that Whitby's picturesque setting and its long and eventful history from conquest to commerce, acted as a lure to writers from near and far. These have included Bram Stoker, Wilkie Collins, Charles Dickens and Lewis Carroll, the latter having spent his childhood days in Richmond, a market town some few miles away in the beautiful Yorkshire Dales. It is these four then, this Victorian 'cream of the crop' writer wise that I will discuss in this article, examining their interaction with the town and what if anything, influenced any of their works that involved 'the supernatural'

They certainly had plenty to influence their fertile imaginations in Whitby, with its strange tales of Bargheist hellhound dogs and ghost coaches that roamed its narrow streets at night, as well as the soul-stealing and terrifying wafts (doppelgangers) that could accost you unawares during your daytime shopping.

Its folklore too provided a literary mine for our writers, much of which probably stemmed from Saxon and Norse mythology. There was the New Moon worship performed by its young girls, anxious to see who their husbands would be and the macabre superstitions of the seafolk, the outcome of their working day or even their possible sudden death, being determined by a chance encounter in the street with a pig, drowned dog or cat, or something as simple as the sight of a woman's face.

The rebuilt HMS Endeavour a symbol of Whitby's seafaring past, at anchor in the harbour

Bram Stoker

A beautiful Goth girl promenading

The first and most famous (supernatural-wise) of this illustrious worship of writers that I will document is of course Bram Stoker. Stoker arrived in Whitby in 1890, staying at 6 Royal Crescent, which is just off the fashionable North Terrace on Whitby's west side. He was known to observe the town below and Abbey opposite, from the nearby Royal Hotel's large windows, possibly holding a contemplative cigar in one hand and with a fine scotch in the other, as he brooded over the movements and motivations of his terrifying creation.

It was when he chose to leave his lair and walk around the vibrant tourist haunt below that he began to bring together the threads he would use to weave his fantastic tale. It was here that he would have observed the well-attired visitors promenading to the sound of the cheerful band on the bandstand, perhaps seeing a Mina Harker here or a Lucy Westenra there, as well as sizing up the local men in their seaman's gear, plucking an obvious Mr Swales from their number.

His thoughts would then turn to undead Balkan vampire lords, who he began to imagine roaming Whitby's streets of the living at night, hunting down the hapless, beautiful and weak. Firstly drinking their life's blood from their warm quivering throats and finally capturing and imprisoning their tormented souls for eternity. An analysis of Stoker's time and movements in Whitby, point to several key areas within the town that helped him form the genesis of Dracula's assault on England.

In 1890, Stoker visited the then Whitby subscription library on the waterfront and borrowed a book titled 'An Account of the Principalities of Wallachia and Moldavia (1820) by William Wilkinson'. Its contents detailed the exploits of a ferocious Romanian warlord Vlad Tepes. Tepes, the scourge and ruthless impaler of the Turks, formed the foundational core of Stoker's character Dracula, who in his undead state was to terrorise the imaginations and dreams of generations of readers to come.

Gradually then and during his continued meanderings in the town, Stoker began to acquire the facets of this part in the story's captivating timeline, which would help him to fill out and bring to life The Count's nefarious character so convincingly. The ship that Dracula steals into Whitby on called the Demeter (in Greek mythology, the name of the goddess of the harvest and an ironic touch here perhaps, with regard to the vampires' infertility), actually relates to a real event that occurred around this time.

In the fictional story Dracula's ship, its crew decimated by his blood lust, is beached on Collier's Hope near Tate Hill Pier. Metamorphosing into a great hound, Dracula quickly escapes the schooner as it shudders to a halt, leaving its dead captain still lashed to its wheel. Once on the nearby pier, he swiftly bounds up the nearby precipitous staircase known as the 199 steps to the wind-blown graveyard above the town.

The dreaded Count Dracula

The real incident that was used by Stoker to put together the Count's unwanted arrival occurred in October 1885 and involved a Russian schooner called the Dmitry (note the similarity in the name). The story of this ship's demise was covered by the local paper, The Whitby Gazette on the 31st of October 1885, its article stating that the ship had been blown into the port on its journey to England from Narva (present day Estonia). The article reads as follows: -

'A little later in the afternoon a schooner was descried to the south of the harbour, outside the rocks. Her position was one of great danger; for being evidently unable to beat off, there seemed nothing for it but to be driven among the huge breakers on the scar. Her commander was apparently a man well acquainted with his profession, for with consummate skill he steered his trim little craft before the wind, crossing the rocks by what is known as the 'sledway' and bringing her in a good position for the harbour mouth.

The piers and the cliffs were thronged with expectant people, and the lifeboat 'Harriot Forteath' was got ready for use in case the craft should miss the entrance to the harbour and be driven on shore. When a few hundred yards from the piers she was knocked about considerably by the heavy seas, but on crossing the bar the sea calmed a little and she sailed into smooth water. A cheer broke from the spectators on the pier when they saw her in safety.

Two pilots were in waiting, and at once gave instruction to those on board, but meanwhile the captain not realising the necessity of keeping on her steerage, allowed her to fall off and lowered sail, thus causing the vessel to swing towards the sand on the east side of the harbour.

On seeing this danger the anchor was dropped, but they found no hold and she drifted into Collier's Hope and struck the ground. She purported to be the schooner 'Dmitry' of Narva, Russia, Captain Sikki, with a crew of seven hands, ballasted with silver sand. During the night of Saturday the men worked incessantly upon her that her masts went by the board and on Sunday morning, she lay high and dry a broken and complete wreck, firmly embedded in the sand.'

Milady Rosemary looks out across Collier's Hope

Stoker's corpse-manned ship is therefore based on this real event, which he probably found out about by either looking in the subscription library's records, or from one of the garrulous old whalers and fishermen of the town. Many of these old salts would have been seen trawling along Whitby's piers during Stoker's stay and their appearance and personalities no doubt formed the basis of some of the characters in his story. Interestingly, there were still many old seamen in the town akin to these mariners when I worked there in the 1980's as The Collector of Dues for the harbour and I like Stoker, used some of their tales for my own book, 'The Whitby Ghost Book' about Whitby's Spirit World.

Those Stoker came across would have helped him conceive and put together individuals within Dracula, such as the likeable and yarn-spinning Mr Swales or 'Sir Oracle' (as Mina calls him), who befriends Mina and the doomed Lucy. These old locals' knowledge of the town's folklore, would have been invaluable to Stoker for filling in details about its supernatural goings-on, such as the 'wafts' and 'boh-ghosts' that Mr Swales mentions. These supernatural phenomena, are in fact based on well known local legends that I used to scare the wits out of tourists with, when I narrated them during my evening 'Supernatural Whitby Walk' in the nineteen eighties.

The Waft for example, is a supernatural entity mentioned in Robinson's 'A Glossary of Yorkshire Words and Phrases Collected in the Whitby Neighbourhood' that was published in 1855, pages 187-188, the extract for it reading as follows: -

'A WAFT, a gliding spectre. " I saw his waft," the semblance of the living person, of whose death the supposed appearance of the waft is said to be a denotation !'

Make no mistake, the waft apparitions that duplicated you in every detail, were soul-stealing killers. If you saw one of them in a shop or in the street, there was only one way of fending it off before it stole your soul and destroyed you. You immediately had to issue a challenge (preferably in the local vernacular) on the lines of, 'What's thou doing here?' 'Thou's after no good I'll go bail, get thy ways yom wit thee, get thy ways yom! In doing this you were saved (hopefully), the waft skulking away to find weaker and easier prey.

The waft is also known by another name to the more academically orientated and that is the doppelganger or 'double-goer'. This word is German in origin, Whitby having had close trading connections with northern Germany right up to the 19th century. The German version has a similar portent of trouble attached to it, though thankfully not as severe as the Whitby version, this being that it is a harbinger of bad luck or perhaps indicating the existence of an evil twin.

The 'boh-ghost' that Mr Swales mentions is also a well-known apparition in Whitby and throughout Yorkshire. In Whitby it's commonly known as 'The Barguest', a huge black hellhound with glowing eyes that stalks Whitby's night-time streets. It is said that if you hear the 'howl of the Barguest', you are not long for this life...gulp! Sound familiar? Of course it does, it's the 'immense dog' in Stoker's novel that 'sprang up on the (ship's) deck from below...and running forward, jumped from the bow (of the stricken Demeter) on to the sand'. It's Dracula, making his escape from the beach at Collier's Hope and haring off up the 199 steps to the suicide's grave on unhallowed ground in the churchyard above. Which quite nicely brings me to the grave that Dracula is said to have inhabited and over which the unfortunate girls favourite bench lay.

The 199 Steps with 'coffin rests' visible up which Dracula, in the form of a monstrous hound bounded

Going up the torturous 199 steps to the church at Whitby, is thigh-stretching agony and it's almost as bad if you take the nearby 'donkey road' directly to the side of it.   As you follow the route that Dracula, in his form of a monstrous hound scampered up, you come across several benches that have an interesting history and usage.   They are seats yes, but also 'coffin rests' that were placed there so that the tired pallbearers taking coffins up to the church could take a well-earned rest.   Their grateful use thus ensured that the pallbearers did not join the departed that they were carrying up in the coffin, when they finally reached the church at the top.

Once in the churchyard, we have a glorious view over the bay from the cliff-side's benches and we can also glance at the stories on the row upon row of tombstones celebrating Whitby's honoured dead.   The departed here, range from ordinary folk to ship's captains murdered by pirates in far-flung lands and Stoker would most certainly have come up here, to see and possibly add details from the tombstones' narratives to his great tale.

A present-day bench by the cliff edge in the churchyard, near the place where the now long washed away one stood and that Stoker probably used in his book

The bench that the girls and Mr Swales sat on during the story and on which he is eventually murdered, would probably have been based on one of the several benches existent on the cliff during Stoker's time. Furthermore, the unfortunate George Cannon's grave on unhallowed ground (**Note.** This Church custom regarding the burial of suicides was practised right up until 1882, when the Church's Canon Law changed, but may well have been carried on for a period afterwards), may also have been taken from the presence of a suicide's grave in that area.

The grave Stoker used would have either been outside the main burial ground and most probably on the graveyard's north side, where all the benches (more or less) face north and directly out to sea as you look out from the harbour's mouth. Since Stoker's time however and due to coastal erosion, the one he probably envisaged as being the one on which the girls and Mr Swales sat, has gone over the cliff a long time ago, though many still ask to this day and much to the local vicar's consternation, 'Where's Dracula's grave?'

Present-day Goth gels using today's more modern, if less genteel form of transport. Mina and Lucy would certainly have escaped the voracious Count's deadly attentions had they but had one of these!

As can be seen then, there was much in Whitby for Stoker to glean, ponder over and use in his fantastic tale. On the subject of characterisation within the story and as I said earlier, Stoker in all probability put together the make up of seaman mentioned as well as other characters in the Whitby chapters, from direct contact with its townsfolk.

For example the surname of our brave protagonist Jonathan Harker, is a local one that Stoker probably came across in the town. I couldn't help but note that the house I bought in nearby Grosmont in the late 1980's, was owned by the Harker family. The lady of the house during the house's purchase mentioned that her ancestor had been a maid in service at Royal Crescent and possibly at the very house that Stoker stayed at.

It seems then that Whitby's ancient setting and fascinating folk, have a habit of conjuring up thoughts of vampires, wraiths and the supernatural in the imaginations of tourists who come to visit Whitby, which brings me neatly to my next writing aficionado, Wilkie Collins.

Wilkie Collins

A depiction of the White Wraith phantom that has been seen in Whitby which Collins may have heard of and included in his famous story

Wilkie Collins' (of 'The Woman in White' fame) illustrious footsteps echoed on Whitby's cobbled streets when he arrived there in August 1861 and it was at Whitby he began to write his novel Armadale.

He did not seek a solitary stay of literary contemplation however and brought with him his lover Caroline Graves, the woman that was his inspiration for the tortured, asylum-bound character Anne Catherick, in the 'Woman in White'. Whilst he and Graves stayed at Whitby's Royal Hotel, the most prestigious there at that time, he wrote to his mother on the 22nd of August about Whitby saying, '…this is one of the most magnificent places in England'.

Not for long however, as Whitby was (and still is) a popular seaside resort. It was with a heavy but not surprising heart then that three weeks later we find him writing to his friend Charles Ward saying, "The noises indoors and out, of this otherwise delightful place (comprising of children by the hundreds under the windows, and a brass band hired by the proprietor to play regularly for hours during the day for the benefit of his visitors), are keeping me back so seriously with my work that I must either leave Whitby or lose time…". Regrettably then, it was exeunt stage right from Whitby (or in this case to the railway station), for Willkie Collins and his lover.

That might be all we could say about Collins and his association with Whitby, 'not a ghost in sight!' I hear you say, save for his fictional white lady. However, as a result of the research I carried out for my book 'The Whitby Ghost Book', local people have told me about at least three instances of white, wraith-like apparitions that appeared on the cliff across the road from the Royal Hotel and in the area between the cliff top and the beach below.

The first of these stories was told to me by a nice old chap who as a boy scout in 1905, was enjoying a campfire on the beach below the hotel with his fellow scouts. He recounted his experience to me in the following words.

'It was in the evening and suddenly as we looked up to the cliff top, we saw a white misty figure - you couldn't tell if it was a man or a woman - floating down the face of the cliff. We ran over to the spot where we thought it would land, but it disappeared the instant before it reached the sand. There was no fog or mist about and to this day we just don't know what it was'.

Extraordinary? Yes, but this was not a sighting by one person, it was a mass sighting by several scouts, and no explanation was ever found for what they actually saw.

The next sighting was in the early nineteen eighties, this time it was a couple out walking their dog at night in the same spot and they saw more-or-less the same white wraith slowly descend the cliff and vanish before it touched the beach below. As the wraith vanished the woman turned to her husband to discuss the apparition's appearance, only to find that he had vanished also! Well not vanished actually, she could see him doing an Olympic sprint down the far end of the beach, too scared to stay with her and doggie (brave fellow) and also too scared to ever talk about it again.

**The beach and in the distance the cliff top from which
the wraith is said to descend**

Last but not least as far as Collins is concerned, we
have an even-stranger, additional manifestation of this wraith
at which I was fortunate enough to be present.

In the late 1980s, I was a member of the local amateur
pantomime company called the Apollo Players and we were
doing our Christmas pantomime 'Aladdin', at the local
Whitby Spa Pavilion Theatre. This was built in the 1870's and
coincidently, it lies on the west cliff and just below the Royal
Hotel. Well, there I was on stage left about to go on as the
devastatingly funny (well I thought so) Wishi McWashi, when
one of the young girls in the chorus asked me to come with
her to look at something strange she had just witnessed and
which had given her quite a fright. We promptly went behind
some props in the area where she said the incident had taken
place and she told to me the following story.

'I was standing here watching the performance, when suddenly a woman all dressed in white came towards me from back stage. I couldn't make out her face but I then noticed she was dressed in a violet crinoline dress (a contradiction from her original description of the woman being dressed in white or perhaps the manifestation's appearance became clearer the nearer she got to the girl?), like the ones you see in Sutcliffe photos (A local Victorian photographer that practiced in Whitby) and her hair was in a bun. I thought she was going to say something to me and for some reason I felt a bit frightened when suddenly, she just turned towards that bit of prop against the wall (it was a painted prop panel made of light wood and painted canvas) and vanished into it!'

I saw that she was a bit shaken and reassured her. Eventually she asked me if I could move the prop aside to see what was behind it, just in case it might give some sort of explanation as to what had just happened. I was happy to do this and moved the relatively light piece further along the wall. Well believe you me I was just as surprised as her at this point, as when I slid the panel to the side a doorway was revealed behind it, which by the look of it had been bricked up for a very long time. Anyway, being the troupers we both were, we took the attitude that the show must go on despite this strange event and carried on with our performance. I did however start using the white wraith's latest manifestation in my Supernatural Whitby Walk from that time on and as I recall it went down very well, especially on particularly dark and misty (these are called a 'fret' in Whitby) nights.

Is there a connection with these strange events to Wilkie and Caroline? Or is it just sheer coincidence, as all the apparitions occurred well after the story's published date of 1859?   Did he leave some imprint of his genius there that continues to perform over the years (a recording ghost)? Or could this be a totally different local apparition of some unfortunate woman (an actress perhaps?) from the area's Victorian past, who leapt or was pushed to her death off the high cliff and is doomed to go through the same fatal event again and again? I know not, but feel free to stay at the Royal Hotel and attend a performance in the Spa Pavilion to see if she graces you with an appearance.

Do please let me know however if she does appear again, so that I can update her spectral visitor's card. Let us now move from leaping wraiths to rabbit holes, as we discuss Lewis Carroll, a writer beloved of children young and old and his sojourn at this supernatural watering hole.

Lewis Carroll

A tearoom in the Market Square called the Walrus and Carpenter adjoining the streets on which Carroll, Dickens, Collins and Stoker would have walked

That well known 'nonsense poem' The Walrus and the Carpenter' from Lewis Carroll's, 'Through the Looking Glass and What Alice Found there' (1871), appears to have been inspired by his long walks along Whitby's beaches, the like of which you have seen in this book's previous pictures. Carroll stayed during his six visits to Whitby (1854-1871) at 5 East Terrace, which is now the La Rosa Hotel and he did so under his real name Charles Lutwidge Dodgson, Lewis Carroll being his pen name.

His visit in 1854 was as a student mathematics lecturer, not a writer (mathematics was one of Carroll's professions) and he was part of a group of mathematicians from Christ Church College Oxford, who were giving lectures in the town.

Whilst he obviously had a vocation in maths, Carroll's heart and imagination seems to have been occupied elsewhere. One of his companions a Thomas Fowler, recalls that 'Dodgson' (Carroll) used to sit on a rock on the beach, telling stories to a circle of eager young listeners of both sexes' and that this seminal experience was in fact the genesis event for Alice's adventures and his future writings.

He did in fact publish his first work at Whitby in 1854, a satirical poem called 'The Lady of the Ladle', this in the local paper which is still going strong today and is called The Whitby Gazette. The poem refers to parts of the town in its verse and mentions the prominent Royal Hotel, which was built in 1849 by George Hudson who was also known as 'The Railway King' and is the same Royal Hotel mentioned earlier in Stoker's and Collins' visit. Here is a verse from it to whet your appetite: -

The Youth at Eve had drunk his fill,
Where stands the 'Royal' on the Hill,
And long his mid-day stroll had made,
On the so-called 'Marine-Parade'

Literary works aside, what then was Carroll's involvement with the world of the supernatural? Well in Whitby alas, not much as far as we know, though he may have been influenced by any one of its superstitions and ghostly tales?

A chilling depiction of Carroll's dreaded Jabberwocky from 'Through the Looking Glass and What Alice Found There' (1871)

However, he was interested in 'the supernatural' and was a member of the Society for Psychical Research, which he joined when it was first formed in 1882 along with another illustrious writer, Mark Twain. He also authored a humorous poem, 'Phantasmagoria' in 1869, which is the most matter-of-factual and endearing 'A-Z of haunting' manual for ghosts that I've ever come across. Here's a sample of it for you from the pinkmonkey.com site, the full poem being available at the following link: -

http://pinkmonkey.com/dl/library1/carol46.pdf

PHANTASMAGORIA

CANTO I

The Trystyng

ONE winter night, at half-past nine, Cold, tired, and cross, and muddy, I had come home, too late to dine, And supper, with cigars and wine, Was waiting in the study.

There was a strangeness in the room, And Something white and wavy Was standing near me in the gloom I took it for the carpet- broom Left by that careless slavey.

But presently the Thing began To shiver and to sneeze:

On which I said "Come, come, my man!

That's a most inconsiderate plan, Less noise there, if you please!"

"I've caught a cold", the Thing replies, "Out there upon the landing." I turned to look in some surprise, And there, before my very eyes, A little Ghost was standing!

The other connection that Carroll has with ghosts and that probably had an impact on his Alice stories, is the story of *'The Little Drummer Boy'*, a story he would almost certainly have heard about when at school in Richmond, in the nearby Yorkshire Dales.

In this story, involving the town's military garrison and set sometime during the 18th century (though no specific date is given), soldiers in Richmond castle find a partially blocked up secret passageway underneath the castle's mighty walls, access seemingly available only via a small hole at the passage's entrance.

Unable to get through it themselves, they ask the regiment's drummer boy if he could squeeze through it with his drum. Being a plucky soul he did this, dragging his drum through behind him. The soldiers then asked him to beat his drum whilst going through the passage's dark gallery and they would listen from the street level above and follow the sound of his drumbeat to wherever this may lead them. He duly marched off and the soldiers scrambled to the surface and began to follow the tattoo he played on his drum.

Suddenly and near the famous old Easby Abbey, his drumming stopped and nothing could be heard. The soldiers cried frantically for him to start his drumming again, but received no answer and he was never seen again.

The mighty fortress that is Richmond Castle in Richmondshire

This well-known story of the ill-fated drummer boy then, was probably an 'itch' in Carroll's imagination, which just had to be scratched in one way or another when the Alice story began to coalesce in his mind, her descent down the rabbit's hole being analogous to the doomed drummer boy's descent into the fatal passageway.

Charles Dickens

The White Horse and Griffin Inn where Dickens dined and still looking much as it did in his day

Last but not least we have the great Charles Dickens, who first visited Whitby in 1836 and who later encouraged his friend and work colleague Wilkie Collins (both of them worked on the periodical 'All the Year Round'), to stay there.

On a later visit to Whitby in 1844, he stayed with the Marquis of Normanby at the Marquis' stately residence of Mulgrave Castle, the large lawn of which was called 'The Quarterdeck' in honour of the fact that Lord Nelson had manfully strode across it.

Dickens apparently and as a homage to Nelson (one assumes) danced a hornpipe on it, which must have been very interesting to watch. The Marquis was a 'Liberal politician, travel writer, novelist and dandy' and it was to his wife, the Marchioness Maria that Dickens dedicated one of his great novels 'Domby and Son' (Tomain, C, 2011).

Whilst at Whitby he also lunched at the very Dickensian looking 'White Horse and Griffin Inn', which is still in a more or less unchanged state to that which Dickens would have seen on his visits. It is a place full of the atmosphere of Dickens' time and I actually considered buying it back in the eighties and opening it as either a museum or ghostly attraction, though it was in a very derelict state then and beyond my finances at that time. It has however been thoroughly renovated now and has a good restaurant according to its reviews.

Today and as in Dickens' time, you can within its antique interior partake of an oyster or two, or perhaps a plate of fine Whitby dressed crab washed down with a glass of champagne, this just prior to going on one of the town's several ghost walks.

What ghost connections then did Whitby have for our final member of this illustrious group, if any? It's hard to say, his biographer John Forster is on record as mentioning that as far as ghosts were concerned, Dickens has "…something of a hankering after them".

For me 'The Signal-man' will always be his most memorable tale of the supernatural, though you may have your own favourite Dickens' tale of the spirit world that you believe to be his best. He was after all a member of the London Ghost Club (established 1862 and now called simply The Ghost Club) and therefore had a keen interest either personally and more important from a literary sense (bringing in the pennies), in the supernatural.

Some direct input into his stories from the area came from his friendship with his friend Charles Smithson, who ran a law practice in nearby Malton. Scrooge's counting house for instance, is based on Smithson's Chancery Lane premises in Malton. It was at Smithson's home at Easthope hall in the same area that he came across a woman who he used to construct the character of the drunken nurse Mrs Sarah Gamp in his novel Martin Chuzzlewit, some of which he also wrote in Malton.

One of Whitby's many old yards, interestingly not the place for an 'argument', but the place where the Argument family once lived

As for any actual supernatural connections with Dickens and Whitby, no definite connections have been recorded…as yet. However, this gives you an excellent excuse to come to Whitby to investigate and prove otherwise, perhaps during one of the upcoming Goth Weekends held every year. During this time of Gothic and Steampunk romping and promenading, you can stroll along its still cobbled streets and seek out its spirit roots (both ethereal and alcoholic), ideally in one of its many old inns, whilst at the same time soaking in the wealth of historical ambiance around you, achieving (hopefully) some supernatural enlightenment.

A very gentlemanly Steampunk strutting his stuff at a Whitby Goth Weekend

I hope fellow delvers into the world of the supernatural that this article has helped inform you on this illustrious group of famed Victorian taletellers and their interaction with this lovely old seaside town. I also hope that it may want you to delve deeper into this mysterious old town's history. To this end, I have provided a more-or-less full bibliography for you to peruse at the end of the article and I welcome any questions you may have about a place I have lived in and still to this day find fascinating, adieu!

Paul Fitz-George, O. A. Dip. (Parapsychology)

Bibliography

Books Researched

Fitz-George, Paul, (2014) *'The Whitby Ghost Book'*, Amazon, eBook Kindle Version, accessible at: - **https://www.amazon.co.uk/Whitby-Ghost-Book-Paul-Fitz-George-ebook/dp/B00E675MBU.**

Feuer, Bryan, (2016), *'Boundaries, Borders and Frontiers in Archaeology: A Study of Spatial Relationships'*, Jefferson, North Carolina, USA, MacFarland and Company Inc.

Baker, William, (2007) *'A Wilkie Collins Chronology'*, London, UK, Palgrave Macmillan.

Thompson, Ian and Frost, Roger, (2016), *'Secret Whitby'* Merrywalks, Stroud, UK, Amberley Publishing Ltd.

McDermott, Paul, (1987) *'The Whitby Ghost Book'*, Leicester, UK, Anderson Publications. (Please note, the author has changed his name to Paul Fitz-George and this book is now available as an e-book on both Kindle and Google Books).

Stoker, Bram, (1897 reprint 1985), *'Dracula'*, Harmondsworth. UK, Penguin Books Limited.

Robinson, Francis, Kildale, (1855), *'A Glossary of Yorkshire Words and Phrases Collected in the Whitby Neighbourhood'*, Soho Square, London, UK, John Russell Smith Publishers.

Wakeling, Edward, (2015) *'Lewis Carroll: The Man and his Circle'*, London, UK, I. B. Tauris & Co Ltd.

Tomalin, Claire, (2011) *'Charles Dickens: A Life'*, London, UK, Hamondsworth, Middlesex, Penguin Books Ltd.

Peach, Howard, (2003) *'Curious Tales of Old North Yorkshire'*, Wilmslow, Cheshire, UK, Sigma Leisure.

Web sites accessed

The Black Horse Inn Webpage 2015-2016, *'Black Horse People'*, accessed 15th July 2016 - **http://www.the-black-horse.com/history/people.html#stoker.**

The Whitby Gazette online, *'Descendant of Dickens to follows his Whitby footsteps'* (July 2014), accessed 15th July 2016 - http://www.whitbygazette.co.uk/what-s-on/descendant-of-dickens-to-follows-his-whitby-footsteps-1-6704372#ixzz4ETw3FcmE.

Endeavour Cottages, *'Whitby and its connections with Lewis Carroll the famous author'* (undated), accessed 15th July 2016 - **http://www.endeavourcottage.co.uk/whitby-blog/lewis-carroll.html.**

Locker, R, *'Out on Ye! Underground Whitby'*, *'Lewis Carroll and the Whitby Adventure'* (April 2010), accessed 15th July 2016 - **http://whitbypopwatch.blogspot.co.uk/2010/04/youth-at-eve-had-drunk-his-fill-where.html.**

Locker, R, *'Out on Ye! Underground Whitby'*, *'A Tale of Two Wrecks'* (October, 2011) accessed 19th July 2016 - **http://whitbypopwatch.blogspot.co.uk/2011/10/tale-of-two-wrecks.html.**

Lewis, P, *'Wilkie's Aldborough'*, (2000), accessed 15th July 2015 - **http://www.web40571.clarahost.co.uk/wilkie/Aldeburgh/Aldeburgh.htm.**

Fitz-George, P, 'English Ghosts - Archives of Doom, 20th October 2015, The Ghostly Beat of the Drummer Boy's Drum', (2016), accessed 19th July 2016 - http://www.englishghosts.com/page10.htm.

Kozlowski, B, *'A Dickens of a Good Ghost Story'* In Historic UK (2016), accessed 19th July 2016 - **http://www.historic-uk.com/CultureUK/A-Dickens-of-Good-Ghost-Story/.**

Brindle, S, and Wilmott, T, *'History of Whitby Abbey, English Heritage'*, (undated), accessed 19th July 2016 - **http://www.english-heritage.org.uk/visit/places/whitby-abbey/history/.**

Brenan, G, and de Fonblanque, E, B, Wikipedia, *'William de Percy'* (2016), accessed 19th July 2016 - **https://en.wikipedia.org/wiki/William_de_Percy.**

(Unnamed author), Wikipedia, *'Doppelgänger'* (2016), accessed 20th July 2016 - **https://en.wikipedia.org/wiki/Doppelgänger.**

Taylor, T, *'The Haunted Museum, The Historic and Haunted Guide to the Supernatural'*, (2003-2008), accessed 22nd July 2016 - **http://www.prairieghosts.com/spr.html.**

Carroll, L, *'Phantasmagoria'*, (1869), at pinkmonkey.com, accessed 22nd July 2016 - **http://pinkmonkey.com/dl/library1/carol46.pdf.**

Davidson, J, (2011) *'A Hankering After Ghosts: British Library's Charles Dickens and the Supernatural'* in *'Culture 24'*, accessed 23rd July 2016: - **http://www.culture24.org.uk/history-and-heritage/literary-history/art370174.**

(Unnamed author), (2012) *'The Ghost Club'*, accessed 23rd July 2016: - http://www.ghostclub.org.uk/history.html.

Printed in Great Britain
by Amazon

44053293R00030